GW00866028

Get the Hat and Tap Tap Tap

PHASE 2

2a

Level 2 – Red

Helpful Hints for Reading at Home

The graphemes (written letters) and phonemes (units of sound) used throughout this series are aligned with Letters and Sounds. This offers a consistent approach to learning whether reading at home or in the classroom. Books levelled as 'a' are an introduction to this band. Readers can advance to 'b' where graphemes are consolidated and further graphemes are introduced.

HERE IS A LIST OF NEW GRAPHEMES FOR THIS PHASE OF LEARNING. AN EXAMPLE OF THE PRONUNCIATION CAN BE FOUND IN BRACKETS.

Phase 2			
s (sat)	a (cat)	t (tap)	p (tap)
i (pin)	n (net)	m (man)	d (dog)
g (go)	o (sock)	c (cat)	k (kin)
ck (sack)	e (elf)	u (up)	r (rabbit)
h (hut)	b (ball)	f (fish)	ff (off)
l (lip)	ll (ball)	ss (hiss)	

HERE ARE SOME WORDS WHICH YOUR CHILD MAY FIND TRICKY.

Phase 2 Tricky Words			
the	to	I	no
go	into		

HERE ARE SOME WORDS THAT MIGHT NOT YET BE FULLY DECODABLE.

Challenge Words			
by			

TOP TIPS FOR HELPING YOUR CHILD TO READ:

• Allow children time to break down unfamiliar words into units of sound and then encourage children to string these sounds together to create the word.

• Encourage your child to point out any focus phonics when they are used.

• Read through the book more than once to grow confidence.

• Ask simple questions about the text to assess understanding.

• Encourage children to use illustrations as prompts.

Get the Hat
and
Tap Tap Tap

Written by
Robin Twiddy

Illustrated by
Alex Dingley

Can you say this sound and draw it with your finger?

Get the Hat

Written by
Robin Twiddy

Illustrated by
Alex Dingley

It is Pat. Pat has a hat.

His hat is big and has bells.

A rat has got his hat!

The rat is in the hat.

Pat runs to get the hat. Puff, puff.

Get the hat, Pat! Duck.

Pat gets his cat, Tom.

Get the rat, Tom the cat!

The cat hit the hat.

The rat is on the mat!

Pat has got his hat back.

The cat has got the rat.

Can you say this sound and draw it with your finger?

Tap Tap Tap

Written by
Robin Twiddy

Illustrated by
Alex Dingley

Ana sat on the mat.

Ana tap, tap, taps on the mat.

Ana got the pan.

Ana tap, tap, taps on the pan.

Ana sat at the tap.

Ana tap, tap, taps on the tap.

Ana got the hat.

Ana tap, tap, taps on the hat.

Ana sits by the cat.

Ana, no! Not on the cat!

Ana sits by the cat. Pat, pat, pat.

Pat, pat, pat on the back.

©2019 **BookLife Publishing Ltd.**
King's Lynn, Norfolk PE30 4LS

ISBN 978-1-83927-277-6

All rights reserved. Printed in Malaysia.
A catalogue record for this book is available
from the British Library.

Get the Hat & Tap Tap Tap
Written by Robin Twiddy
Illustrated by Alex Dingley

An Introduction to BookLife Readers...

Our Readers have been specifically created in line with the London Institute of Education's approach to book banding and are phonetically decodable and ordered to support each phase of the Letters and Sounds document.

Each book has been created to provide the best possible reading and learning experience. Our aim is to share our love of books with children, providing both emerging readers and prolific page-turners with beautiful books that are guaranteed to provoke interest and learning, regardless of ability.

BOOK BAND GRADED using the Institute of Education's approach to levelling.

PHONETICALLY DECODABLE supporting each phase of Letters and Sounds.

EXERCISES AND QUESTIONS to offer reinforcement and to ascertain comprehension.

BEAUTIFULLY ILLUSTRATED to inspire and provoke engagement, providing a variety of styles for the reader to enjoy whilst reading through the series.

AUTHOR INSIGHT:
ROBIN TWIDDY

Robin Twiddy is one of BookLife Publishing's most creative and prolific editorial talents, who imbues all his copy with a sense of adventure and energy. Robin's Cambridge-based first class honours degree in psychosocial studies offers a unique viewpoint on factual information and allows him to relay information in a manner that readers of any age are guaranteed to retain. He also holds a certificate in Teaching in the Lifelong Sector, and a post graduate certificate in Consumer Psychology.

A father of two, Robin has written over 70 titles for BookLife and specialises in conceptual, role-playing narratives which promote interaction with the reader and inspire even the most reluctant of readers to fully engage with his books.

PHASE 2
2a

This book is an 'a' level and is a red level 2 book band.

Additional images courtesy of Shutterstock.com. p.18 – Arizzona Design, Ivan Dubovik, doyata, openeyed, Nadya_Art, MchlSkhrv, Sudowoodo